Trevor

Adventure in the Country

New edition! Revised and abridged

By Laura Lee Hope

Illustrations by Pepe Gonzalez

Publishers · GROSSET & DUNLAP · New York

Revised and abridged by Nancy S. Axelrad.

Copyright © 1989 by Simon & Schuster, Inc. All rights reserved. Published by Grosset & Dunlap, Inc., a member of The Putnam Publishing Group, New York. Printed in the U.S.A. THE BOBBSEY TWINS is a registered trademark of Simon & Schuster, Inc. Library of Congress Catalog Card Number: 88-80425   ISBN 0–448–09072–4
A B C D E F G H I J

Contents

1 Aunt Sarah's Secret 1
2 The Piano Ghost 12
3 Major Trouble 24
4 Missing Evidence 34
5 Dead-End Clue 42
6 Lost and Found 52
7 Wild Rocket 59
8 A Scary Escape 67
9 Little Detectives 76
10 Tricky Thieves 84
11 Bert's Ordeal 93
12 Double Returns 100

■ 1 ■
Aunt Sarah's Secret

"Open them!" exclaimed six-year-old Freddie Bobbsey. His blue eyes darted to the two envelopes his older sister, Nan, was holding.

"Hurry! Hurry!" Flossie said with a toss of her blond curls. She was Freddie's twin.

"Okay, okay." Nan grinned. She tore the flaps and pulled the letters out quickly. She read for a minute, then all of a sudden her smiling face went blank. "That's strange."

"What's the matter?" Bert asked. He and Nan were twins, too. They were twelve and had dark hair.

"See for yourself," Nan replied. She handed him the letters.

With a little gulp he read them aloud to the other children. Both letters were from Aunt Sarah. She and Daniel Bobbsey, the twins' uncle, lived on a farm near the village of Meadowbrook. Their son, Harry, was the same age as Bert and Nan.

"I love Meadowbrook Farm!" Freddie said when Bert finished reading.

"So do I!" Flossie added. "I love the horses and the chickens and the cows. Are we going right away?"

"Not so fast, you two," their brother broke in. "One letter says we can. The other says we can't because Aunt Sarah and Uncle Daniel are leaving on a trip this Saturday."

The small twins moaned.

"I can't believe it," Nan declared. "I can't believe they don't want us to come."

"No?" Bert replied.

"Look at the postmarks on the envelopes." Bert took a quick glance. "The second letter was sent first and the first letter was sent second."

Flossie blinked. "Huh?"

Nan explained that Aunt Sarah's invitation was mailed after the other letter telling about the change in plans.

"You know," Bert said, "these signatures do look different."

Taking another glimpse, his twin sister agreed. "We'd better call Aunt Sarah," she suggested.

"Let's tell Mommy first," said Flossie.

Nan agreed. The twins pounded upstairs but walked quietly down the hall to their mother's room.

Nan tapped gently on her mother's bedroom door. "May we come in, Mom?" she asked, taking a step inside.

"What is it, honey?" Mrs. Bobbsey answered.

Nan told about the puzzling arrival of two letters from Aunt Sarah and that they thought they should call her.

Mrs. Bobbsey went to the phone and dialed her sister-in-law's number.

"Sarah," she said, "this is Mary. . . . Fine, and you? . . . Sarah, did you send the twins two letters?"

The children stood quietly, waiting for the answer. There was a long pause before Mrs. Bobbsey spoke again.

"Uh-huh. I'll tell them, Sarah."

"What's going on?" Freddie whispered to Nan.

"Sh," Bert said. "They're still talking."

But in a little while Mrs. Bobbsey called her older daughter to the phone. "Aunt Sarah wants to speak with you."

"Hi, Aunt Sarah," said Nan. "You do? . . . Oh, yes, very much!"

"What's going on?" Freddie asked again.

3

This time Bert shrugged.

"I was right!" Nan said, hanging up the phone. "Aunt Sarah *does* want us to come!"

"So she didn't send the other letter," her twin replied. "Hmm."

"No, she didn't."

"I don't suppose she knows who did," Bert continued.

Nan shook her head.

"Which means somebody doesn't want us to go to Meadowbrook Farm!" Freddie blurted out. The remark sent Flossie running into her mother's arms.

Bert frowned. "I wonder why not."

"Well, while you're wondering about that," Nan said with a twinkle, "I'll be wondering about Aunt Sarah's surprise."

"Surprise? What surprise?" Flossie asked.

"It's a secret!"

When the twins' father came home that evening, they told him all about the invitation. "We can go, can't we, Daddy?" Flossie prodded.

"Of course you can go. I just wish I could. But I have a lot to do at the lumberyard this week." He hiked Flossie onto his shoulder. "But I'll come as soon as I can. How's that?"

Flossie laughed. "Okay, Daddy," she said.

The next few days were very busy as the children got ready for the trip. Aunt Sarah had asked the twins' mother if the Bobbseys' house-keeper, Dinah Johnson, could come with the family to help out. Mary Bobbsey said of course, and Dinah was eager for the change of scenery. It was decided that they all would fly to Wells-town, the nearest city to Meadowbrook with an airport, and Mr. Bobbsey would drive the family van up when he came.

"We have to take Snoop too," Freddie re-minded his mother. Snoop was the black cat that had been given to Freddie after the little boy had been locked in a department store by mis-take.

Mrs. Bobbsey looked doubtful. "I don't know if that's such a good idea."

"But we have to! Snoop rescued me. We can't leave him here all by himself!"

Seeing the desperation in her son's face, she finally gave in. "He has to go in the carrier, then."

"He won't like that," Freddie said. He remem-bered the first time he and his mother had taken Snoop to the veterinarian in Lakeport. When they tried putting Snoop in the big plastic case with air holes, he almost escaped.

"Well, I'm afraid he doesn't have a choice, honey," Mrs. Bobbsey said. "We can't take him on board with us. He'll have to go with the bag-gage."

Early Friday morning Dinah's husband, Sam, brought the van around to the front of the house. He and Mr. Bobbsey and Bert helped load the suitcases and the cat carrier, which was too big for anyone to hold. Then the family and Dinah piled in, and Sam drove them to the airport.

Although the flight to Wellstown took less than an hour, Freddie spent most of it worrying about Snoop. But when the boy saw Uncle Daniel and Harry, he forgot his worries entirely. "There they are!" Freddie shouted. "Come on, Flossie!"

The children ran toward the man, who was tall and athletic-looking like their father.

"Hello, hello," he said, giving them both a hug. "You remember Harry."

His son grinned. "Hi, Freddie. Hi, Flossie."

"Hi, Hal!" the twins chorused in unison, using their nickname for Harry. By now the rest of the travelers had also joined the group.

The village of Meadowbrook was not far from Wellstown Airport, and in a short while after collecting their baggage and Snoop, Uncle Daniel drove everyone to the farm in a van much like the one in Lakeport. It was a pleasant ride through long stretches of tilled land. It ended at a narrow lane, bordered by thick

6

hedges of boxwood, that led to the driveway of the family's big clapboard house.

When the van finally rolled to a stop, a side door opened. Short, plump Aunt Sarah was waiting to meet the visitors. After greetings were exchanged, the twins' aunt said, "Now go upstairs and get settled."

"But hurry back!" Harry urged. "I want you to see Major."

In a few minutes the children had changed into T-shirts and blue jeans and were romping down the stairs again. Following Harry, they ran across the emerald-green lawn toward the big barnyard. In a separate pen next to the white barn was the prize bull. He snorted and swung his head up and down when Harry introduced him.

"He wants to play with us!" Freddie said merrily.

"Not so fast," his brother warned. "Bulls can be dangerous."

Reluctantly Freddie left Major and followed Harry and the other children back to the barnyard. "This is Frisky," Harry said. He walked up to a little black-and-white calf that was tied to a stake near the barn. As he stroked her, the animal rubbed her head affectionately against his shoulder.

"May I ride her?" Freddie asked.

"You don't ride calves," Harry explained, "only ponies and horses."

"Oh . . . uh, can I take her for a walk?"

"Silly," Flossie said, giggling. "No one takes calves for a walk."

But while Bert and the girls went with Harry to see the horses, Freddie lingered behind. Impulsively he slipped the rope off the stake and put the loop around his wrist.

"Come on, Frisky," he said. "You'd like to take a walk, wouldn't you?"

The calf went along quietly until she caught sight of the open gate and the green lawn beyond. She kicked up her back heels and made a dash, dragging Freddie behind her.

"Stop, Frisky!" he pleaded. "I can't run so fast!"

His cries reached the ears of his mother and Aunt Sarah, who were talking on the porch.

Aunt Sarah ran down the steps. "Let go, Freddie! Let go!" she shouted.

But the loop was tied fast around the boy's wrist, and he could not get it off. Frisky charged behind a small tree, winding the rope as she went.

Whoops! Freddie fell to the ground, and the rope slipped over the calf's head, letting her skitter away happily.

At the same time, the other children had heard the commotion, too, and ran to the barn door.

"What's Freddie doing with that calf?" Bert asked, completely baffled.

"Frisky's running away with him!" Harry exclaimed, dashing in pursuit.

But by the time he reached the front lawn, the calf had broken loose and Freddie was being led into the house. Flossie darted after him while Harry and the older twins looked to see where the calf had gone. She was standing in the vegetable garden, munching on some tender young shoots.

"Hey, Frisky, don't do that!" Harry commanded.

At the sound of his voice, the animal bounded away, this time toward the barn.

"Whew!" Bert said. "It looks as if she's finally ready to go home."

But Bert was mistaken. The runaway calf sprinted across the pasture and into a thicket that grew around it.

"Come on!" Harry said, bolting after her. When the trio reached the spot, they could hear the animal thrashing through the brush. Then suddenly the thrashing stopped. There was a moment of silence followed by a loud *splash!*

"What was that?" Bert asked.

"I think Frisky jumped into the river!" Harry replied.

"Can she swim?" Nan said anxiously.

"I don't know. I hope so," Harry said.

The little group weaved through the tangle of bushes and tall grass until they reached the riverbank. The calf was nowhere in sight.

"Maybe that noise was from something else," Harry said encouragingly. "I see a tree limb floating downstream. It could've been that. Let's hunt along the shore."

But even though the searchers pushed on through the dense overgrowth, they found no sign of Frisky anywhere.

■ 2 ■
The Piano Ghost

"Maybe Frisky circled back to the barnyard," Nan said hopefully.

But when the children returned to the area, the calf was not there. Disappointed, they went up to the house. Freddie, who now had a bandage around his wrist, was waiting outside with Flossie.

"Did you catch Frisky?" Freddie asked eagerly.

"No," Bert said, shaking his head. "She just disappeared."

Freddie looked away. "And it's all my fault."

"Don't worry about it, Freddie," his uncle replied. "She'll turn up. And if not, I know where I can get another calf."

But try as he might, Freddie could not stop thinking about it. Where had Frisky gone? Would she be all right? Nan tried to take Freddie's mind off the calf by mentioning the mysterious letter the twins had received.

"Did you bring it with you, dear?" Aunt Sarah inquired. "I'd like to see it, if I may."

"It's in my bag," Nan said, excusing herself.

Uncle Daniel looked at his wife with questioning eyes. "It seems that someone wrote to the children, telling them not to come," she explained, "and signed my name to the letter."

"Nan figured it out right away," Bert stated proudly.

"Figured what out?" his uncle asked, more perplexed.

"That the letter wasn't from Aunt Sarah."

As Bert spoke, Nan reappeared with the letter. She spread it on the kitchen table in front of her aunt and uncle.

Without another word Uncle Daniel took a pair of eyeglasses out of his shirt pocket and put them on. "If I didn't know better, I'd think this was your signature," he said to his wife.

Peering at it more closely, she admitted, "It *is* a good forgery."

Nan related the twins' confusion when two letters had arrived from Aunt Sarah on the same day. But then she noted the postmarks on the envelopes and realized what had been done.

"Has anything unusual happened at the farm?" Nan asked.

"Recently, you mean?" her uncle said. "No, nothing that I'm aware of."

"Frisky disappeared," Freddie interposed.

"Now, you stop fretting over that calf," Aunt Sarah told the boy. "Frisky can take care of herself just fine."

She studied the letter again, then gazed wistfully at the wooden bird feeder outside the kitchen window. All morning it had been filled with small chickadees. Now it was empty except for a brilliant red cardinal that had shooed the other birds away.

"Saaarrah," her husband said, snapping his fingers in front of her blue eyes.

"Oh," she said, startled, "excuse me. I guess I was daydreaming."

Flossie snuggled under her arm. "Do you still have a surprise for us, Aunt Sarah?" she asked boldly.

"I sure do. It's coming tomorrow, or I should say I'm taking you to it tomorrow."

"Oh, goody!" the little girl exclaimed.

As her aunt cast a knowing smile at the twins' mother, Mary Bobbsey winked in return. Now everybody except Freddie was smiling.

His mouth was set in a frown. "Uncle Daniel,"

14

he began, "maybe Frisky went to another farm. Is that possible?"

"Maybe she went to visit her cow friends!" Flossie giggled.

The children's uncle patted both their shoulders. "You could be right," he said. "Harry, how about making a few phone calls for your cousins?"

"Sure, Dad," the boy replied.

At once he put in calls to all the farmhouses within a radius of three miles. No one had seen Frisky. He was ready to quit, when his father suggested he try Mr. Holden.

"Doesn't he live in Wellstown?" Aunt Sarah asked.

"Yes, but I suppose if Frisky is frisky enough, she could go to Wellstown," Uncle Daniel said.

As he spoke, his son looked up the phone number and dialed. In a moment he was describing the runaway calf to his listener.

Suddenly the boy's eyes lit up. "What happened, Mr. Holden?" he asked. "Oh, no. . . . Oh, how awful. . . . Do you want to talk to Dad?" He handed the receiver to his father.

"Has he seen Frisky?" Freddie inquired.

"No, he hasn't." But before Harry could explain, the phone conversation ended abruptly.

15

There was a stony expression on Uncle Daniel's face as the other man clicked off.

"Some of Ed Holden's cattle are missing," he said. "They disappeared during the night. The police were over there all morning investigating."

"How could cattle just disappear?" his wife asked.

"Maybe the same way Frisky did," Freddie observed.

Uncle Daniel rubbed his chin thoughtfully. "The cattle were put in a big truck and driven away."

Nan's brain was spinning. "Someone broke into Mr. Holden's farm and stole his cattle?"

"That's what he said."

"Any leads?" Bert inquired.

"Only tire tracks, nothing else. The police are doing an investigation now."

Nan glanced at the mystery letter on the kitchen table. Whoever had written it did not want the twins anywhere near Meadowbrook. Just who was it? A cattle thief? Maybe, or maybe not, she thought, putting the letter in her pocket.

That night everyone slept fitfully. Flossie dreamed that Frisky came prancing into the house and began to play the piano in the living room! Smiling to herself, the little girl awoke.

Then suddenly she sat up in bed and listened. The house was dark, but someone *was* playing the piano!

"Nan! Nan!" Flossie jumped out of bed and tugged at her sister's covers.

Sleepily Nan lifted her head off the pillow.

"Somebody's playing the piano!" Flossie whispered.

Nan stumbled from her bed and followed Flossie into the hall. They paused. The first floor was dark, and everything was quiet.

"You must have been dreaming," Nan said, "but I'll get Uncle Daniel anyway, and we'll look."

Sleepy-eyed, the girls' uncle emerged from his room. He turned on the lower-hall light and hurried the girls to the living room. As they suspected, no one was there. But Nan noticed that a sheet of music that had been on the piano rack now lay on the floor.

"Somebody obviously knocked it down," she said. "Flossie, was this the tune you heard?" she asked jokingly, holding up the sheet music.

Flossie frowned. "It was more like lots of scales."

Uncle Daniel smiled politely, and Flossie knew he thought she had been dreaming, too. She did not mention Frisky as he turned out the lights, and they all went back upstairs.

When the girls were in their room once more, Flossie said, "Nan, I *did* hear the piano—really I did."

"Maybe there's a ghost in the house," her sister replied, getting into bed.

"You think so?" Flossie cringed, pulling the covers up to her chin.

"Go to sleep, Floss. We have a big day ahead of us tomorrow."

The next morning everyone was up early. Aunt Sarah puttered about the kitchen with Dinah while Mrs. Bobbsey and the children set the table for breakfast.

"Mmm, something smells delicious," the twins' mother said.

"Pancakes and homemade sausages," Aunt Sarah replied, "just the way you like them."

"And plenty of real maple syrup," Dinah added.

When they were all seated, Aunt Sarah spoke up. "I'm taking you to an auction today," she said.

"What's an auction?" Flossie asked.

"Well, it's a public sale of different things. And people who want to buy them tell the auctioneer how much they're willing to pay."

Still puzzled, Flossie looked at her uncle.

"An auctioneer sells the item to the person

18

who offers to pay the most," Bert explained, letting his uncle swallow the rest of his coffee.

"Are we ready?" Uncle Daniel asked. He stared at the half-eaten breakfast on the children's plates. "If we want to sit up front, we have to leave soon."

Not another word was spoken until the meal was over. Then all the Bobbseys hurried into the van for the short trip to town. They parked on the square, where a tent had been erected on the green. At the far end was a raised platform with a small table behind which stood a man holding a wooden gavel.

"Is he the awk-shneer, Aunt Sarah?" Flossie asked.

"Yes, he is, dear. And those are the things for sale." She nodded toward the articles near the platform. There were tables and chairs, antique lamps with faded shades, and stacks of dishes and glassware.

After the auctioneer began his opening speech, Aunt Sarah whispered to Nan, "There's something very special your mother wants to buy."

As she spoke, the tent buzzed with conversation, and the gavel pounded for attention. "Ladies and gentlemen," the auctioneer announced, "the next lot is something wonderful indeed."

Nan looked expectantly at her aunt. "Is this it?" she asked.

The woman smiled.

There was a stir as a man led a pretty golden-colored pony to the front of the platform. He was harnessed to a basket cart.

"Isn't he cute?" Flossie squealed.

The other children in the audience thought so, too, and they clapped in delight.

"Now, who will start the bidding for this beautiful palomino pony?" the auctioneer said.

A tense moment of silence followed until Mary Bobbsey raised her hand, making the first bid. Almost immediately, a hand shot up from the other side, making a higher bid. Then another hand went up, followed by a fourth.

The twins looked at their mother as she watched the auctioneer lift his gavel. Again Mrs. Bobbsey raised her hand.

"Oh, Mommy!" Flossie exclaimed, thinking they had won the pony.

But the other bidders jumped in, tripling the price quickly!

Mrs. Bobbsey confided to Uncle Daniel, "Dick and I didn't plan to spend this much."

Then she noticed the row of disappointed faces next to her. She barely heard the auctioneer when he said, "Going, going . . ."

"Wait a minute!" she shouted, a bit flustered.

The twins held their breath as their mother made one more courageous bid, and a hush fell over the crowd.

"Do I hear more, ladies and gentlemen?" the auctioneer said. "This palomino is a real beauty."

He surveyed the audience with a glance at the other bidders, who sat quietly, and then pounded the gavel hard. *"Gone!"* the auctioneer exclaimed with a nod at Mrs. Bobbsey.

"Wowee!" Freddie cried.

"Congratulations, Mary!" Aunt Sarah said.

After Mrs. Bobbsey paid the auctioneer, she told the twins that Aunt Sarah had learned of the pony sale through a neighbor and passed the news to the Bobbseys right away.

"That was my secret!" Aunt Sarah confessed.

"But of course ponies and carts aren't allowed on the streets of Lakeport," the twins' mother went on. "So you'll have to leave yours on the farm at Meadowbrook."

"Whenever you come to visit, you can play with Rocket all you like. We'll take good care of him for you," Aunt Sarah remarked.

"He's waiting for you outside," Mrs. Bobbsey said.

"May Nan and I drive him back?" Bert asked.

"You may, but don't go too fast. We'll ride ahead with Uncle Daniel and meet you at the farm."

After the others had left, the older twins climbed proudly into the front seat. Bert took the reins.

"Go, Rocket!" he called.

The little pony trotted obediently out of town and along the road leading to Meadowbrook Farm.

"Isn't this great?" Nan said, enjoying the warm gentle breeze against her face.

Then suddenly one of the wheels slid over a pothole, jolting the cart. Bert pulled back on the reins, but it was no use. Part of Rocket's harness had broken, allowing the pony and cart to separate abruptly.

"Rocket!" Nan cried, watching the reins slip away. The palomino paid no attention. He trotted farther and farther away.

23

■ 3 ■
Major Trouble

As Nan and Bert watched the pony vanish down the road, they let out a long discouraged sigh. "Now what?" Nan asked her brother.

Ignoring the question for the moment, he kept his eyes on Rocket while Nan climbed out of the cart. "He's turning off the road," Bert said.

"That's odd. I wonder where he's going."

"I don't know, but let's find out."

The twins examined the cart briefly, then pulled it off to the side of the road and hurried in the direction that Rocket had gone.

When they reached the turn, they discovered it was a narrow lane leading to a small farmhouse with red shutters. "Where are we?" Nan asked, looking around.

At that moment a gray-haired man in overalls stepped out of the barn. "Are you looking for me?" he asked the twins.

"I don't know, sir," Bert said. "I mean, we're looking for our pony. His name is Rocket. He's a palomino."

"Oh, I see. You wouldn't be Daniel Bobbsey's nephew and niece, would you?"

"Yes!" the girl said, her brown eyes popping wide. "I'm Nan, and this is my brother Bert."

"Well, I'm Mr. Burns. Glad to meet you. Rocket used to belong to my grandchildren. They moved away, so I told your aunt and uncle I was putting him and the cart up for sale." He smiled at the visitors. "So you're the new owners. Wait right here."

Before the children could reply, he ducked into the barn again. They heard a soft whinny, then Mr. Burns calling Rocket's name.

"Rocket!" the twins exclaimed.

They ran into the barn as the elderly farmer finished turning the pony around. "I guess Rocket doesn't realize this isn't his home anymore," Mr. Burns said with a chuckle.

Nan threw her arms around the pony's neck. "Oh, Rocket," she said, stroking the silky white mane.

"Now all we have to do is get the cart," Bert commented.

"I was going to ask you about that," Mr. Burns said. "Did you have an accident?"

"Not exactly. We were riding along, when all

of a sudden we hit a pothole and the harness broke," Nan explained. She showed where Rocket's breast collar had split apart.

Taking a closer look, the farmer clucked in dismay.

"I guess it was cracked already," Bert said.

"This harness was in good condition when I brought it to the auction," the man replied, checking the rest of the straps. "These were cut."

As he talked, an expression of fear crept into the twins' eyes. If Mr. Burns was right, then someone had tampered with the cart on purpose! But who?

Instantly Nan blurted out, "The letter."

"Letter?" the farmer inquired, petting Rocket.

She told about the mysterious forged letter the twins had received.

"So you think the sender may have done this," Mr. Burns concluded.

"Precisely," Bert agreed. "We have an enemy in Meadowbrook."

"Well, now, don't go letting your imagination get the better of you," the man cautioned. "You won't find a nicer place than Meadowbrook." Deciding not to discuss the matter further, the children nodded. "Now, tell me where the cart is and we'll hitch up Rocket." Mr. Burns took another harness from the corner of the barn and put it in a small trailer.

In a little while everyone, including Rocket, was on board. They sped down the main road until they reached the cart.

"We really appreciate your help," Bert said, watching Mr. Burns adjust the second harness. The pony whinnied and wiggled his ears.

"So does Rocket." Nan laughed.

"Now, don't you give them any more trouble, Rocket boy," the farmer said as the twins climbed into the cart. This time Nan took the reins. "Easy does it, missy."

"Thanks, Mr. Burns," she said, flicking the reins gently. "Come on, Rocket. Gotta go home." Mr. Burns gave a light slap on the flank and the pony cantered obediently up the road.

"Are we lucky!" Bert said. "After losing Frisky, I'd have hated to tell Mom we lost Rocket, too."

"And I'm glad we didn't get hurt," Nan replied. "If Rocket had been going faster when the harness broke, we would've been."

A few moments later the Bobbsey driveway came into view. As the cart pulled in, Harry ran from the farmhouse to greet them. He looked very upset.

27

Thinking it was because of the twins' delay, Bert said, "Wait till you hear this!"

But Harry wasn't listening. "Our bull, Major, has been stolen!" the boy announced.

"Not Major!" Bert said in shock.

Harry explained that he had fed the prize animal that morning and left him in his pen. "When we got back from the auction I went out to check on him and he was gone!"

"Did Dinah see any strangers around?" Nan asked immediately.

Harry shook his head. "She was in the kitchen and didn't hear a thing."

"I'm really sorry," Bert said in a sympathetic tone.

"Dad is talking to the state troopers on the phone now."

"Two mysteries in one day," Nan remarked with a sigh. "That's a lot."

Harry asked about the other one, prompting the twins to describe their own mishap.

Before they finished, however, Freddie and Flossie had raced out to join them, along with the rest of the family. "Did Harry tell you about Major?" Freddie questioned. "Isn't that terrible?"

"The worst," Bert answered.

Later, when two police officers arrived, they

tried to figure out how the theft had occurred. The children listened in fascination.

"I'd say a truck came up through the field back of the barn and carried the bull away," Lieutenant Kent said. "That would explain why Mrs. Johnson didn't hear it in the house."

"These could be the thief's shoe marks," Bert offered. He pointed to some indentations in the ground that ran alongside hoofprints out to the field.

The officer knelt over them. "You're right," he said. "The bull must've been driven up a ramp into the truck."

Nan, meanwhile, had picked up a pocket notebook with the initials CM on it. "Maybe this is a clue to the thief's name," she said excitedly, handing it to the second officer, whose name was Pfister.

"Could be. Thank you." He flipped the pages, but nothing had been written on them. "I'll take it along as possible evidence."

Before he and the other man left, however, Nan revealed what had happened to her and Bert that morning. They retrieved the broken harness from the back of the cart and showed it to the investigators.

"Maybe you'd better show them that letter, too," Mrs. Bobbsey said worriedly.

"Good idea, Mary," her sister-in-law remarked, sending Nan into the house.

When she returned, Bert was in the middle of explaining about Aunt Sarah's forged signature.

"Has anything else happened that we ought to know about?" Lieutenant Kent asked, pocketing the letter.

"Frisky ran away," Freddie replied.

"That's our calf," Uncle Daniel said. "We haven't been able to find her."

"Maybe she was stolen, too," Flossie suggested.

The policeman wrote a note on the back of a blank card. Then he and his partner left.

Afterward Freddie asked sullenly, "Bert, do you think they'll catch the thieves very soon?"

"They could, I suppose."

"But do you think they *will*?"

Bert sighed. "I don't know, but I sure hope so."

That evening everyone waited for good news from the police, but none came.

Early the next morning Bert went to the barn to feed Rocket. He paused in front of Major's empty pen, then walked on to the stall where the little palomino pony was standing quietly.

"Hello, Rocket," Bert said, stroking his neck. "Good fellow." Rocket nuzzled Bert. Bert speared some hay and tossed it into the box.

For a while the only sound Bert heard was that of the hungry pony—until something rustled in the hayloft above. He glanced up just in time to see a tousled black head draw back.

"Who's up there?" Bert called.

"Just me," came a small voice.

"Well, come down right away," Bert said sternly.

A little boy about Freddie's age climbed slowly down the ladder. He had big soulful brown eyes and wavy black hair to which bits of straw clung.

"Who are you? Where did you come from?" Bert asked, scanning his rumpled clothes.

"My name is Johnny Hernandez. The bus went off without me."

"What bus?"

"The bus that takes us to camp," Johnny said, his stomach growling. "I'm hungry."

"Well, follow me. You can have breakfast with us," Bert said. "Then you can tell us what happened."

The boys entered the dining room to find everyone else seated. All eyes looked at them in astonishment.

Bert introduced his companion. "This is Johnny Hernandez. I found him in the hayloft."

Dinah put a big bowl of cereal in front of their guest. Freddie and Flossie watched him in-

31

tently as he ate. When he finally put down his spoon and reached for a glass of milk, Flossie asked, "Where do you live?"

"New York. But I was on my way to camp when I got off the bus."

"Were you going to Camp Horizon?" Uncle Daniel inquired.

"Yes," Johnny said, swallowing the rest of his milk. "There was something wrong with the bus, and the driver stopped to get it fixed. I went down under the bridge to look at the water. But when I climbed back up, the bus was gone."

"So you walked here," Aunt Sarah said.

Uncle Daniel pushed back his chair. "I'm going to call the camp."

"You can ride in our pony cart if you want to," Flossie told Johnny, "and help us solve our mysteries."

"You've got mysteries?" the boy asked.

"Frisky disappeared first," Nan said, noting his puzzled look. "She's a calf."

"And our prize bull, Major, was stolen while we were at the auction today," Harry added.

Johnny sat forward, his eyes snapping with excitement. "Was the bull in the same barn where you found me?" he asked.

"Did you see him?" Bert replied.

"Yeah, and I think I know who took him!"

33

■ 4 ■
Missing Evidence

Johnny continued his story. "When I went into the barn, I had heard an animal snorting and pawing at the floor. I was too scared to go near him. I just climbed the ladder and went to sleep in the hay. When I woke up, I heard two men talking about the bull. I thought they lived here, and I didn't want them to find me, so I kept real still."

"Did you see them?" Nan asked eagerly.

"No, I was too afraid to look. But I heard them say they were going to take the bull away."

"Where?" the children said at the same time.

"I don't know."

"Did the men call each other by name?" Harry said.

Johnny twisted his face in a frown. Then he burst out, "Mitch and— It was a funny name." He paused. "Oiler, that's it!"

"Oiler?" Freddie repeated.

"Yeah, like that stuff that poured out from under the bus."

Bert looked at his uncle, who had come back to the table. "Do you know anyone around here with those names, Uncle Daniel?" he asked.

"As a matter of fact, your aunt said a guy named Mitch came to the house one day when Harry and I were out."

"He was alone," Aunt Sarah explained. "He was looking for work, so I gave him a few chores to do. That was all. He was here only a few hours, and I must say he did a good job, too."

"What did he look like, Mom?" Harry asked.

"Oh, sort of heavyset, shorter than your father. He had a cap on, so I didn't see the color of his hair, but he had brown eyes. That I do remember."

"I'll give the information to Lieutenant Kent," Uncle Daniel said.

Harry smiled hopefully. "Major is supposed to be in the County Fair. If we get him back soon," he said, "he could win an award."

"Well, first things first," his father reminded him. "We have to take Johnny to camp. The director is waiting for him."

The younger twins pouted. "Can't he play with us?" Freddie asked.

"Not today, sweetheart," Aunt Sarah answered for her husband. "Maybe tomorrow.

We'll have to get permission from the camp."

"Tomorrow's the Fourth of July!" Flossie shouted.

"There will be speeches and a band concert on the village green at eleven o'clock," Uncle Daniel said. "Would you like to go with us, Johnny?"

"Yes, sir!"

"Let's have a parade," Bert said.

"That'd be fun!" His younger sister clapped her hands. "We can dress up!"

"And march into town," added Harry. "But what'll we wear?"

"How about paper hats?" Nan suggested. "Red-white-and-blue ones!"

"We've got everything you need," Aunt Sarah said.

As she rose from her chair, however, her husband interrupted, "I have another idea. Why don't we continue this discussion on the way to the camp?"

Bert said, "I think I'll stay home and work on my costume." He watched the other children leave. He picked up his costume but soon put it down and went to explore the field where the theft had occurred. He located the trail of tire marks, but to his surprise, the hoofprints had completely vanished. Perplexed, he followed the tire marks into the brush. Then he circled back, going in a slightly different direction. On the way he found an identical set of tire marks but still no hoofprints.

"This is weird," Bert said to himself.

He retraced his steps several times, looking for the clue that had mysteriously vanished. Suddenly he caught sight of something glistening in the grass and hurried toward it.

It was an electric-blue ball-point pen. Bert guessed it belonged either to one of the state troopers or to one of the thieves. "I bet it fell out of the little notebook Nan found," Bert thought.

As he turned it over, he discovered printing on the side of the pen. Several of the letters, however, were worn off.

"O-u-n," Bert said aloud, "e-r. Oun er."

Part of the space between the two syllables appeared smooth and flawless, which led the boy to conclude they were part of two words, not one long one.

"Oun er," he repeated, sticking the pen in his pocket.

The hot summer sun beat on his face as he squinted at the woods beyond the field. He looked back at the farmhouse. There was still no sign of Uncle Daniel's van, which meant the others had not yet returned.

He pulled out the pen again, then stuffed it

back in his pocket and ran toward the barn. Observing his mother sound asleep in the porch hammock, he decided not to disturb her.

"I can be back before she wakes up," he concluded, working fast to hitch Rocket to the pony cart.

But as he started onto the main road, Uncle Daniel's van pulled toward him. "Where are you going?" Uncle Daniel asked.

"To town. I found another clue to the thieves, but I'm not quite sure what it means."

"What is it?" Nan inquired.

"It's a pen with some letters on it," Bert revealed.

"What about the parade?"

"This won't take long. Want to go with me?"

Nan declined. She had promised to help the younger twins make costumes.

"I'll go, Bert," Harry volunteered, hopping out of the van.

After the others had driven away, Bert told about his investigation of the field. "That's when I found this," he said, showing Harry the blue pen. "I'd like to know where it came from."

The other children, meanwhile, set to work on their parade hats.

"I want to be Uncle Sam!" Freddie announced.

"All right, you be Uncle Sam," Nan said. "We'll make you a top hat to wear with the red-and-white-striped pajamas you brought."

"Who can I be?" Flossie asked eagerly.

"You can be Miss Liberty," came the older girl's reply. "You'll wear a crown of gold paper and a white nightgown."

"You know what?" Freddie said.

"What?"

"You should ride Rocket!" her brother exclaimed.

"With you two standing up in the cart! It'll look like a float," Nan said, "sort of."

Dinah, who had been listening to the children's conversation, posed the next question. "Where are the other boys going to sit?"

As the three Bobbseys looked blankly at each other, Bert and Harry had already parked the pony cart and were strolling through the center of Meadowbrook.

"What are you looking for?" Bert's cousin asked.

"For the name that was printed on this pen," the boy detective said.

"How do you know it came from here?" Harry asked.

"I don't," said Bert. "But it's worth a try."

They looked up and down the street. There

were several stores on both sides. Harry noted a luncheonette called Molly's Kitchen, as well as a laundromat with an unpainted sign.

Bert spelled out the word *laundry*. "It's close," he said, checking the letters on the pen. "But this says *o-u-n*, not *a-u-n*."

"Maybe the old sign was spelled incorrectly," Harry said, "and that's why they're putting up a new one."

His companion gave him a long, disbelieving glance and raised his eyebrows. "I doubt it, but we can ask anyway."

Bert showed the pen to the clerk at the counter. "Do you give away pens like this?" he inquired.

"No, we don't."

"Do you know anyone in town who does?"

The young woman shook her head. "Sorry."

After Bert and Harry left, Bert said, "Let's split up. You take this side of the street and I'll take the other, okay?"

"Okay."

As Bert departed, his cousin wandered down the block. Both of them kept their eyes glued to the store signs overhead.

"Town Deli," Bert muttered to himself. "*O-w-n*. Where is *o-u-n*?" he said, passing the delicatessen.

Next came Meadowbrook Hardware and a

40

place called Hamburger Haven. "Hamburger! *E-r!*" the boy thought excitedly. But the position was reversed, and the other word didn't match.

By now Harry had caught up to Bert on the other side of the street. "Did you find anything?" Harry asked.

"No, Hal," Bert said. "Did you?"

"No. I think we ought to go home."

"Give me fifteen minutes. I'll meet you over there." Bert indicated the pony cart, which stood parked on a side street.

Harry kicked the dust off his sneakers and walked toward Rocket while his cousin disappeared across the green. There were more stores with more signs, but not one of them fit the printing on the pen.

Farther up the block, however, was a parking lot that connected with a place Bert could not see. He ran toward it as two cars swung in off the road. For an instant he thought he recognized Lieutenant Kent in one of them, and waved. But the man ignored him, forcing Bert to conclude he had been mistaken.

He drew nearer to the lot. Now he could see the entrance to a diner as well as the sign posted next to it.

"Country Diner! *O-u-n e-r!* That's got to be it!" Bert thought.

■ 5 ■
Dead-End Clue

Excited, Bert darted up the front steps of the Country Diner and went inside. Except for the waitresses and a few people at the counter, the boy saw no one he recognized. He glanced at the booths and wondered about the driver who looked like Lieutenant Kent. Where was he sitting?

Then Bert started toward the waitress behind the counter. She was squirting whipped cream over a strawberry sundae.

"What can I get for you?" she asked Bert after serving the ice cream. "If you like sundaes, ours are the best!"

Momentarily distracted, the boy took a seat. He was hypnotized by the mountain of fresh ripe strawberries. If only Hal had come with him. They could have had sundaes together.

"Homemade ice cream," the waitress continued, seeing the look on his face.

"Um, I'd like two sundaes. Strawberry, please."

"Two?"

"To take out."

The waitress hurried to a freezer compartment while Bert dug into his pocket for the blue pen. Then he noticed an inky point poking out from behind a small pastry case and reached for it. To his disappointment, it was different from the pen he had found. This one had a felt tip, and nothing was printed on it.

When the waitress finally returned with the order, he showed her the ball-point. "Do you know if this diner ever had pens printed up?" Bert asked.

"Not that I know of," the woman said, "but I only started working here a week ago."

"Is the manager around?"

"He's in the back. Do you want to talk to him?"

"If you don't mind."

As she headed for the kitchen Bert swiveled on the stool. Suddenly he saw three men emerge from a table in the adjoining room. To his delight, one of them was Lieutenant Kent.

"Officer Kent!" Bert called.

The man, who was out of uniform, was talking to his companions and pulling out a wallet at the same time.

"Officer Kent!" Bert repeated. He grabbed his ice-cream bag and hurried toward the cash register.

"Bert Bobbsey?" the policeman said, turning in his direction.

"Yes, sir. I waved to you before, but I guess you didn't see me."

"I guess not," the lieutenant said with a glance at his companions. "This is my day off. Sorry."

"I have something to show you." Bert fumbled for the pen. "I found this behind the barn."

As he talked, the waitress emerged again from the kitchen. No one was with her.

"Hey, kid," she shouted to Bert, "don't forget your bill."

The boy nodded.

"I figure the pen belongs with that little notebook my sister found," Bert told the officer.

"Actually, it's mine," the man replied briskly. "Thanks."

Stunned, Bert watched him pay his bill. "Sir, do you know who the thieves are yet?"

"No, but when I find out, I'll give you a call."

The other men, who wore short-sleeved shirts and cotton slacks, sidestepped their companion. "Come on, let's go," one of them barked impatiently. "We've got work to do."

As the trio stepped through the door, Bert

44

hurried after them. "Major's hoofprints are gone!" he said.

To his bewilderment, the lieutenant seemed uninterested and walked away. At the same moment, Bert saw Harry through the vestibule door and dashed outside.

"Hey!" the waitress called, racing after him with the check. Sheepishly Bert skidded to a halt and ran back.

Harry caught up to him. "What's going on?" he asked, puffing hard.

"I just talked to Lieutenant Kent. I showed him the pen."

"And?"

"He says it's his!" Bert announced.

"I figured that pen was a dead-end clue."

Saying no more, Bert paid the bill and followed his cousin outside again. "Detectives have to keep cool under pressure. Here." He gave Harry one of the strawberry sundaes.

When they finally returned to the farmhouse, they found the other children at the dining-room table, surrounded by paper hats.

"We made tricorns for both of you," Nan told her brother, "like George Washington used to wear."

"What about Johnny?" Freddie asked.

"I'll make a tricorn for him, too," Nan said.

Freddie beamed proudly and put on the colorful hat. "I look just like George Washington!" he exclaimed, making Flossie grin.

"I wish I *were* George Washington. I'd have a whole army to help find Major," Harry grumbled.

"What happened in town?" Nan inquired. She cut several pieces of ribbon and made a big bow for Rocket to wear.

"That looks bee-yoo-ti-ful," Flossie said, giving Bert no chance to reply.

Nan gave a smile of satisfaction. "May I have the glue, please?" she continued, then glanced at Bert. "So? I thought you were going to tell us what happened."

"Well, I—" he started to say.

"Daddy's coming tomorrow," Freddie interrupted.

"He is? Great!" Bert said. "Now . . ." He leaned over the table. "Are you going to listen or not?"

At once everyone stopped working. But when Bert finished his tale of woe, Nan said, "So nothing happened."

"Not exactly nothing," Bert replied. He told about Lieutenant Kent's lack of reaction to the missing hoofprints.

"Well, you said he had work to do. Maybe he was in a hurry," Nan put in.

"But he said it was his day off."

"Well, how can that be, if he had to go to work?" Freddie asked.

"I don't know," Bert admitted. "Maybe he does something besides policework."

Bert said no more about it until the next morning, when his father arrived. After thanking him for the new pony, the twins told him everything that had occurred so far.

"You have been busy," he said. "I'm sorry to hear about Frisky and Major."

Freddie looked solemn as Nan put the tall red-white-and-blue hat on top of his head.

"Stand up straight," she instructed her little brother. "Shoulders back, and march!"

Grinning, Freddie began to strut.

"That's it!" his older sister praised him.

Word of the surprise float had spread quickly as the two Bobbsey families, Dinah, and Johnny Hernandez—whom they had picked up early that morning—reached the edge of town. Flag-waving boys and girls and their parents now lined the parade route.

"There they are!" someone cried, seeing the cart.

The children glowed as the band began to play, and others fell into step behind them. Bert, who was walking alongside Rocket, puffed out his chest and led the cart past the square to a decorated platform where the mayor stood.

"You've helped make this day extra special for us," the mayor said, thanking them.

At the end of the celebration, when everybody stood to sing the national anthem, he came to the edge of the platform.

"Before you all leave our beautiful town," he boomed over the microphone, "I have an important announcement to make."

"I wonder what it is," Nan whispered to Bert.

"Reports have been coming in daily about missing livestock," the mayor said. "I don't have to tell you what a serious matter this is for our farmers. If anyone here has any information whatsoever, I urge you to contact Officer Kent at state-police headquarters."

As the speech came to an end Harry looked at the twins anxiously. "I hope everything's all right at the farm. The last time we were away, Major was stolen!"

To everyone's relief, Harry had worried unnecessarily. When they returned, the farmhouse and the barn were just as they had left them. Nothing had been disturbed.

Almost immediately Uncle Daniel asked Johnny, "Have you ever been on a hayride?"

"No, sir."

"Would you like to go on one?"

"Oh, yes!" the boy exclaimed.

While Uncle Daniel harnessed two horses to

an old wagon filled with sweet-smelling hay, Dinah and Aunt Sarah prepared baskets of food for them to eat along the way. There was a lot of laughing and teasing as everyone, including the grown-ups, climbed into the wagon. Mary Bobbsey, who had brought along a big straw hat, stuck it jokingly on Flossie's head.

"I can't see!" the little girl protested as the hat sank over her eyes.

Johnny lifted the brim. "Boooo!" he said, making a funny face and letting the brim go.

Soon Uncle Daniel turned the wagon onto a narrow road that wound through the woods. Although the afternoon was very hot, it was shady and pleasantly cool there.

"There's a good picnic area past those trees," he told his passengers, pulling the wagon to a halt.

While he unhitched the horses, Aunt Sarah and Mr. and Mrs. Bobbsey carried the food to the clearing. The children ran ahead to spread out the long picnic cloth.

"Dee-lish," Nan said on seeing the big platters of crisp fried chicken.

Next came mountainous bowls of creamy potato salad and coleslaw, along with rolls, breadsticks, potato chips, deviled eggs, pickles, and celery stuffed with cheese.

"Okay, everybody, dive in!" Aunt Sarah said.

She opened a thermos of milk and passed cups to the hungry children.

When they finished eating, Aunt Sarah presented two cakes—one covered with a lemon-and-coconut icing and the other with shiny dark chocolate.

"Dee-lish!" Flossie said, imitating her sister.

Freddie quickly downed a slice of each cake and sprawled back on the ground. "I'm full!" he said regretfully. "I can't eat any more."

"Neither can I," Nan said. "Let's play hide-and-seek."

"Yeah, let's!" her sister agreed.

Nan covered her eyes, giving the other children time to disappear among the trees. "Ready?" she asked.

Her eyes open now, she caught a glimpse of Johnny behind a low bush. Soon the rest began dashing from place to place, trying to get "home-free."

"Where's Flossie?" Nan asked after everyone else had been brought in.

"Probably still hiding," Bert said.

"Flossie!" Nan called in vain. "I wonder where she is."

"She went that way, I think," Johnny spoke up. He pointed toward the trees.

Harry heard him. "The cliff's over there!" he exclaimed. "She could've fallen on the rocks!"

■ 6 ■
Lost and Found

Nan turned pale. "A cliff!" she cried, racing through the woods with Bert and the other boys close behind her.

When they reached the craggy edge, they stared at the treacherous slope below. A few feet down, sitting among a pile of rocks, was Flossie! She was crying.

"Are you hurt?" Nan called out.

"No," the little girl said, still weeping.

"Try to climb up," Bert suggested.

"I can't. The stones are too roll-y."

Harry hurried back to get the adults.

"We'll have to make a human chain," Uncle Daniel said, joining them. With him were Richard Bobbsey and the two women.

As the rescuers held hands, Bert edged his way toward Flossie and put his free arm around her shoulders. Not a word was spoken until the rescue was complete.

Afterward Mrs. Bobbsey asked, "Flossie, are you sure you didn't hurt yourself?"

The young girl rubbed her eyes. "I'm sure," she said, explaining, "I wanted to go down the hill only a little way, but I slid."

"It's a good thing you didn't slide to the bottom," her uncle observed as her father picked her up.

Walking toward the clearing again, Harry thought he detected a movement in the woods and stopped. "Do you see anything over there?" he asked Bert.

"No, but I hear a noise. Maybe it's an animal."

As he spoke, a big lumbering animal appeared through the trees.

"It's a cow!" Harry exclaimed.

Stealthily he and Bert crept forward. "There's a tag in her ear," the second boy said, reading it. "She belongs to Mr. Burns!"

"I wonder how she got all the way over here," Harry commented.

"Maybe the cattle thieves tried to steal her, but she got away!"

"Too bad we can't put her in the wagon," Harry said. "We ought to take her back to Mr. Burns."

He took hold of the cow's halter and headed toward the clearing. Bert followed, slapping the animal now and then to guide her.

Upon seeing the boys, Uncle Daniel creased his brow. "There's no grazing around here," he said.

"She belongs to Mr. Burns," Harry said. He indicated the ear tag while Bert offered his theory about the animal's escape from thieves.

"The Burns farm isn't far from here," Uncle Daniel remarked. "Maybe half an hour on foot. Why don't you walk her over there?"

The cow shook her head aimlessly as a fly swooped over it.

"We'll pack up and meet you," Aunt Sarah said, tossing the soiled plates into a plastic bag. "Now, go ahead."

The boys spoke little as they walked. A light wind carried the scent of a freshly cut field. It wasn't long before Bert recognized the lane running next to it—the one Rocket had rediscovered after the harness broke.

As the cousins drew nearer to the Burns farmhouse, a woman ran to meet them. After introducing herself as Mrs. Burns, she asked, "Now, where on earth did you find Bessie? She has been missing since yesterday! We've been so worried about her. She's one of our best milkers, you know."

"We found her in the woods," Harry replied.

"We were having a picnic," Bert said.

The cow lifted her head and mooed.

"What about your other cows, Mrs. Burns?"

"They're all here, if that's what you mean."

"I have a hunch someone wanted to steal all of them," Bert replied, "and had time to take only one. Fortunately Bessie escaped." After putting the cow back in her stall, he and Harry asked permission to search the barn for clues.

"Go ahead," the woman said, "but I don't think you'll find much. I didn't."

Before the boys were done, however, Uncle Daniel's wagon pulled into the lane. He and Aunt Sarah talked to Mrs. Burns, which gave the boys a few more minutes to complete the investigation.

Afterward Nan observed her brother's long face. She could tell he had found nothing of importance.

Johnny tugged on his sleeve. "You'll catch them someday," he told Bert, trying to console him.

"Someday," Bert groaned. He leaned back on the soft hay and listened to the quiet, steady hoofbeats of the horses pulling the wagon while Freddie and Flossie sang.

They stopped as the Bobbsey farmhouse came into view.

"All set, Johnny?" Uncle Daniel asked the boy. "It's time to go back to Camp Horizon."

"Oh, please let Johnny stay a little longer," Freddie begged.

"Please!" Flossie said.

"I promised I'd have him there before sundown," Uncle Daniel said.

Johnny blinked sadly. "I had a great time anyway!" he said, trying to be cheerful. "'Bye!"

That night, when the families were sound asleep, Nan awakened with a start. Someone was playing the piano again, exactly as Flossie had described it—just scales!

The girl lay still and listened. Now all was silent again. "I must've been dreaming," she thought.

But the sound repeated itself. Someone *was* downstairs, and he or she *was* definitely playing the piano. The notes started in little runs but ended with an eerie discordant *thump*.

Nan clutched her blanket. "I'm going to get Daddy and see who's playing the piano," she decided.

She slipped on her robe and slippers and knocked at her parents' door. When her father came out, she told him about the mysterious music.

"I don't hear anything," he said.

"It just stopped, but it may start again."

The pair stole silently down the stairs. When

they reached the living room, Mr. Bobbsey switched on a light. Nobody was at the piano. They walked from room to room but found nothing unusual. Snoop was curled up snugly in his box in the kitchen.

"Maybe it was a mouse," her father remarked.

"Dad, mice aren't heavy enough to push down the keys."

"Not even big fat ones from the field?"

Although Nan wasn't positive, she figured there could only be two possibilities. The mysterious musician was either a ghost—or an intruder!

The next morning she reported the incident to the others. Like everyone else, Flossie had slept soundly and had not heard the noise.

"Do you think the ghost will come back?" she asked.

"If he does," Uncle Daniel said, chuckling, "maybe I can catch him before he gets away."

"How?" Flossie asked.

"By his sheet!" Her twin snickered.

"Oh, so you think this is a pretend ghost," Uncle Daniel said.

Freddie bobbed his head.

"Personally, I don't know what to think," Nan muttered. "But it gives me the creeps."

"Me, too," her sister said.

"Well, I know how to get rid of the creeps,"

Aunt Sarah said. "We have some chores to do. Any volunteers?"

"Me!" Freddie said, raising his hand.

"Me!" Flossie exclaimed.

"We'll be glad to do anything, Aunt Sarah," Bert said, speaking for Nan as well.

"Good. Let's start with the vegetable garden. It needs to be weeded so we can plant seeds for winter carrots and beets."

While the girls did this, the boys elected to clean the stables and put in fresh straw along with hay and water. When they finished their work, they went to the picnic table, where Dinah had set a tray of glasses and a pitcher of lemonade.

From the corner of his eye Harry noticed a gawky-looking boy coming up the driveway. "Oh, no," he said.

"What's the matter?" Bert asked.

"Mark Teron."

"Who's he?"

"The biggest pest I know," Harry replied.

"I know what you mean," said Bert. "Only ours is called Danny Rugg."

Harry wondered what the boy wanted, but whatever it was, it would probably mean trouble for him and Bert!

■ 7 ■
Wild Rocket

As Mark Teron walked into the yard, he announced that he had come to see the new pony. "My dad's going to buy me one if I like it."

Harry eyed the boy warily and let Bert introduce himself. "Follow me," Bert said, leading the way into the big white barn.

"Got a visitor, Rocket," Bert called cheerily.

"Let's put a saddle on Rocket and ride him around the yard," Mark proposed.

"Okay," Bert agreed. "You go first, Hal."

While Harry picked up the small saddle, Bert led Rocket into the sunlight.

"We need stirrups, too," he said, sending his cousin back to the barn.

When Harry returned, he found the saddle firmly in place. He adjusted the stirrups and mounted. At once Rocket reared into the air and shot across the yard!

"Whoa, Rocket! Whoa!" Harry cried, almost

falling off the saddle. "What's the problem?"

Harry felt as if he were being shaken to pieces. He pulled on the reins as hard as he could. But the pony refused to slow down. He galloped out of the barnyard and into the pasture.

Bert and Mark ran after him, yelling, "Whoa! Whoa!"

Strangely, this only seemed to make the animal go faster. The two boys halted.

"Now where's he going?" Bert asked, watching Rocket race past the orchard.

"Please don't run over Trimble's corn!" Harry pleaded, closing his eyes fearfully.

Mr. Trimble's farm bordered the Bobbseys' along the northwest field. He was an unfriendly elderly bachelor who lived alone in a weather-beaten farmhouse. His corn was his special pride.

"Yikes!" Harry shouted as Rocket dived forward, trampling several plants.

In a flash the rider steered his pony to a low fence, but Rocket refused to jump. He stopped so abruptly that the boy jetted over his head and landed in the pasture on the other side.

Lying there for several seconds, he watched a flock of crows circle overhead. Then, as Bert and Mark raced toward him, he slowly picked himself up.

"Are you all right?" Bert asked anxiously.

"Fine. The wind just got knocked out of me, that's all. We'd better run before Trimble sees us."

Bert grabbed Rocket by the bridle and led him back to the Bobbsey property. "I wonder what made Rocket act like that," the boy said. He paused and felt under the pony's saddle.

"It was this!" he exclaimed, displaying a bur. Something about the smirk on Mark's face made Bert ask, "Did you do this?"

Without a word, Mark started to flee. But Harry was too quick for him. He grabbed the boy by the arm and swung him around.

"He asked you a question!" Harry challenged.

"I didn't know Rocket would run away," Mark whined, shaking off Harry's hand. "It was a joke!"

"Some joke," Bert said. "It wouldn't have been too funny if Hal had gotten hurt."

"And just wait till old man Trimble finds his corn broken down," Harry said angrily.

"He probably won't even notice it," Mark scoffed, and walked off.

But Mr. Trimble did notice the damage and stormed angrily to the Bobbsey farm that afternoon. His ruddy face was set in a scowl as he strode across the yard where Uncle Daniel was repairing a barn lock.

"Where's that kid of yours?" he demanded loudly.

Daniel Bobbsey straightened up. "If you've come about your corn, I'll be glad to pay you for any loss."

"People have no business letting animals run wild on other people's property," Mr. Trimble replied briskly.

"It was an accident," Uncle Daniel said patiently. "The pony ran away, and my son couldn't control him."

Harry and Bert saw the crotchety man talking to Uncle Daniel and joined them. "I'm sorry about your cornfield," Harry apologized. "Only a few stalks were knocked over."

The visitor stopped scowling. "I've had nothing but trouble since two of my farmhands left," Mr. Trimble explained. "Mitch and Clint were pretty good with the cows, but I couldn't depend on them to stick around when I needed them. So I fired them last week."

"What did you say their names were?" Bert asked excitedly.

"Mitch LeBeau and Clint Millwood. Do you know them?"

The boy shook his head while Uncle Daniel told about the loss of their bull and what Johnny had overheard in the barn.

"One of the men's names was Mitch," Bert

said. "He called his partner Oiler. Do you recognize the name?"

"Now that I think about it, Clint did have a nickname. I just called him Clint, though."

"Well, his initials fit the ones on a notebook my sister found in my uncle's field."

"Do you have any idea where they went?" Uncle Daniel asked.

"No, I don't."

"How about a picture?" Bert inquired.

"No."

"A sample of handwriting?"

"No," the man said again. "You know, you sound just like a detective."

Bert smiled and nodded. "I want to find Major so my cousin can take him to the County Fair. Maybe you can think of some clue to give to the police."

Mr. Trimble cupped his chin in his hand. "The only thing I can think of are handkerchiefs."

"Handkerchiefs?" Bert repeated.

"Big colored ones—bandannas. Mitch always carried a couple of them. Once in a while he'd wear one around his neck."

"Uncle Daniel," Bert said, "may I call state-police headquarters and tell them?"

"Yes, go ahead."

The two boys hurried to the house and put in

the call. But when Bert asked to speak to Lieutenant Kent, he was told the officer was no longer on the case.

"What's the matter?" Harry asked.

Mystified, the other boy said, "He quit."

"What about Pfister?"

Just then, the other officer came on the line and Bert gave his report. Hanging up the phone, he turned to Harry again. "I guess they don't have any real leads yet."

"None?" his cousin said, arching his eyebrows.

"All he said was thank you."

Later, as they walked into the kitchen, Dinah greeted them with an astounding announcement.

"I heard that piano ghost! And I have proof somebody was in the living room when everybody was outside."

The boys instantly rounded up the other children, who were playing in the yard. They huddled around Dinah to learn the details about the ghostly piano playing.

"You heard it, too?" Nan queried.

"I sure did."

"Oh, Dinah," Flossie said.

"Somebody ran up those keys like this." The housekeeper made a fluttering movement with her fingers. "I have proof."

Flossie and the others looked at her in awe.

"What kind of proof?" Freddie asked.

The small twins hovered next to Dinah as she explained that she had been alone in the house, in the kitchen. "When I heard the piano playing, I was kind of scared to go look for that ghost."

"I would have been scared, too," Flossie said.

"But then," Dinah continued, "I told myself there was nothing to be scared of, so I went back to the room." She paused to look at her admiring audience.

"And then what happened?" Bert asked.

"I found fingerprints!"

Flossie's mouth dropped open.

"Fingerprints," Dinah repeated, "right on the keys!"

The whole group raced into the living room to look at the telltale marks. There they were, just as the housekeeper had described them—small brownish smudges. Harry hurried to get a magnifying glass so that each of the children could look closely at the evidence.

All but the older twins were baffled. Bert and Nan winked at each other. "Let's keep it a secret," she whispered, and her brother nodded.

▪ 8 ▪
A Scary Escape

The next morning when the children came to breakfast, Aunt Sarah looked worried. "Mrs. Burns just phoned me. Her husband took ill last night. Now they can't get their beans picked."

Nan spoke up at once. "We can do it!"

"That's very thoughtful of you, dear," she said. "But you can't handle the job all by yourselves."

"I'll ask Chris and Greg to help us," Harry said.

When he phoned them, the two boys accepted quickly. In a short time they arrived, wearing old faded jeans and T-shirts.

"Didn't you bring sun hats?" Aunt Sarah asked.

"No, Mrs. Bobbsey," Chris said.

"I'm sure I have enough for all of you," the woman said, excusing herself briefly.

A little while later the five boys and two girls set out on foot for the Burns farm.

Upon hearing why they had come, Mrs. Burns said, "You are the dearest, sweetest children I know. Wait till I tell my husband. I'll get the truck and drive you down to the field."

In a few minutes she backed a pickup truck out of the garage, and the children climbed in. When they reached the field, she said, "Now, each of you grab a bushel basket." She pointed to several stacks in the truck.

Then she showed the children just how to snap off the bean pods without pulling up the plants. "Don't pick any beans smaller than this," the farmer's wife said, holding up a pod as an example.

Bert and Harry took the first two rows next to each other as Chris and Greg took the next two. Then came Nan with the small twins. They all set to work, and for a long time no one spoke. The beans were plentiful, and the baskets were filled quickly.

Presently Flossie exclaimed, "We're finished!"

Mrs. Burns, who had been helping, too, straightened up. "Can you carry the basket to the truck, or are you tired?"

"We can carry it. Flossie and I are going to pick a million trillion baskets of beans!" Freddie boasted.

The woman laughed as they each took a handle of their basket and started toward the truck. But the load was awkward and Freddie stumbled. Down they both went, overturning the container as they fell! Beans flew in all directions!

As Flossie got to her feet, she wailed, "Now we have to pick the same beans twice!"

Nan hurried to help, and soon all the beans had been recovered. The older boys, meantime, carried their baskets to the truck, took empty ones, and resumed picking until those were full as well.

Now and then the children stopped to rest. By the end of the morning, Nan looked up at the sky. The noontime sun was directly overhead.

"You're the best workers we ever had," Mrs. Burns complimented the children. "I bet you're hungry, too, right?"

Everyone said yes and followed her to the truck for the ride back to the house. When lunch was over, Mrs. Burns offered to drive the children home.

"No, thanks," Harry said. "We can walk. I know a shortcut, if you don't mind letting us climb your back wall."

"I don't mind," the woman said. "Go right ahead."

She thanked her helpers profusely and led them to the back door again.

"Follow me," Harry ordered, striking out across the yard.

When they finally reached the stone wall that snaked behind a field, they climbed over it and headed across the adjoining pasture.

The next moment Bert cried out, "Look! There's a bull loose! Maybe it's Major!"

As the bull trotted toward them Harry stared at the animal for only a second. "That's not Major!" he exclaimed. "Run!"

Nan grabbed Flossie's hand while Harry caught Freddie by the arm. They dashed across the field, with the other boys at their heels.

"Over the fence! Quick!" Harry called.

All at once Bert's ankle turned and he went down. The others did not see him stumble. They scrambled up over the wall.

"Bert!" Nan screamed, suddenly realizing he had slipped behind. "Hurry!"

As her brother picked himself up he saw the bull charging straight toward him. The image of a brave bullfighter flashed into his mind. Thinking fast, he jumped aside as the animal lunged fiercely, giving him just enough time to race to the wall. The bull turned to attack again, but the boy was already safe on the other side.

"Whew!" Bert said, sinking limply to the grass.

"That was close," Chris said. "You could've been badly hurt."

"I'm sorry the bull wasn't Major," Harry replied shakily.

"Is Major lost?" Greg asked Harry.

Realizing that he had not told his friends about the theft, Harry explained.

"Who'd you say the thieves are?" Chris asked, looking at Bert.

"We're pretty sure they're two farmhands named Mitch LeBeau and Clint Millwood. Clint's nickname is Oiler."

"Well, I think I saw them," the towheaded boy said excitedly.

"You did? Where?"

"I went fishing the other day. Over at the pond above the Burns place, not far from the dam. I dropped my pole in the water and it floated away. I ran after it, figuring I could grab it at the foot of the dam." Chris took a breath.

"And?" Harry urged.

"Standing there—"

"At the foot of the dam?" Bert interrupted.

"Yes, right there I saw two men. They were yelling at each other. The water was coming over the dam pretty loudly, but I did hear a lit-

72

tle bit of what they were saying. They called each other Mitch and Oiler."

"What else did they say?" Harry pressed him.

"I only heard a few words, not whole sentences. They said 'sell' and 'long wait' and . . . and 'smart kids.'"

"Nothing about my bull, Major?" Harry continued.

"I didn't hear anything about him. When the men saw me, they ran away into the woods beyond the dam."

The twins were thrilled with the new information. Without hesitation, they cut across the field after Harry and his friends. In the distance was a stream that ran all the way to the dam.

"How long a walk is it?" Bert asked, feeling a twinge in his ankle.

"Not too long," Harry assured him.

When they saw the dam at last, Bert was overwhelmed by its size. "You don't suppose Major was brought here for a drink and something happened to him?"

His cousin admitted that it was possible. "Major is smart, but he could have broken a leg on these stones and drowned."

"Let's assume he's fine," Nan put in. "Okay?"

The boys agreed. "We'll look for hoofprints," Freddie said.

"And footprints, too!" Flossie chirped.

The children began a thorough search. They found many animal tracks, but none of them had been made by a bull. Troubled, Harry suggested they wade across the stream and check the other side. The others agreed and took off their shoes and socks.

"I don't see any hoofprints," Greg said after a while.

"None whatsoever," Chris remarked.

Neither did Harry or the twins. They were about to give up, when Nan noticed something.

"Come here!" she cried out. "I just found shoe prints. Two sets of big ones!"

"They look like men's," her brother observed. "Let's see where they go."

The young detectives traced the prints to a road that ran deep into the woods.

"The men must've had a truck," said Bert. "See the wide tire tracks?"

"And Major was probably in it," Harry commented. "Maybe Mitch and Oiler went to the brook to get water for him."

Now the children began following the tire tracks. They seemed to go on forever. Finally Harry said they were getting farther and farther away from the Bobbseys' farmhouse.

"It's almost dinnertime, too," Nan said. "We'd better go home."

The others nodded in agreement. Leading the way, Harry took a shortcut through the woods that brought them quickly to the entrance of Meadowbrook Farm.

"Hope you find Major," Greg said as he and Chris waved good-bye. "We'll be around if you need us."

Harry reported the clue to the police, then waited hopefully for news of the thieves' capture. Sadly, none came.

"Those men—and Major—must be very well hidden," the twins' father said.

"They probably know everybody's looking for them," Bert put in. "Which means we may never solve the mystery!"

■ 9 ■
Little Detectives

Bert's pronouncement stunned everyone, especially the other twins.

"Don't say that, Bert," said Nan.

Harry looked at the floor. "He's right," her cousin said. "We may never find Major."

By the time the children finished talking, the evening sky was full of dark clouds. Aunt Sarah peered at the trees blowing in the wind.

"There's a bad storm coming up," she said, hurrying to close the windows.

A few minutes later the clouds burst, and rain poured down in heavy torrents. It rained hard all night and was still coming down the next morning when the twins awoke.

"What'll we do today?" Flossie asked at the breakfast table. "We can't do any 'tective work."

"I know. Let's play in the barn!" Harry suggested. "We'll make a chute-the-chute!"

The small twins were delighted. When they

got to the barn, they climbed to the loft while Harry looked around for a wide plank. There was one near Rocket's stall. Bert helped him prop one end of the plank in the hayloft and the other in the wagon, which stood nearby.

"It's too steep," Harry decided. "We have to move the wagon forward a little bit."

Together the boys pushed the old hay-filled wagon until the plank was less slanted.

"I'll slide down first," Harry said.

He climbed up to the hayloft and crouched on top of the board. Then, pushing against the floor, he started off. With a *swoosh* he slid down the plank into the mountain of sweet fluffy hay.

One after the other all the children tried the makeshift slide. The barn rang with their shouts and laughter.

"This is fun!" Flossie said.

"Just one more ride," Harry announced finally, as the little girl stepped onto the board again.

To everyone's horror, she whizzed down so fast she made a somersault and landed with a *whack* against the side of the hay wagon.

"Flossie!" Nan shrieked, and jumped into the wagon.

Immediately the little girl began to sob. "I hurt."

"Where?"

"Everywhere," she said, uncurling her small chubby legs.

As Freddie and Harry stood by silently, Bert climbed into the wagon to help. He and his sister laid Flossie out flat on the hay and asked her to raise each arm and leg slowly.

"Easy does it," Bert encouraged her. The little girl obeyed. "Good, Flossie, good."

She smiled wanly. "I'm okay," she said at last.

By late afternoon the rain had stopped, but the sky was gray as lead.

"I wonder how Johnny's camp held up under the storm," Aunt Sarah said, looking at the mud puddles that swelled across the yard.

"Maybe we should call to find out," Bert said.

"I will. Right now."

When Aunt Sarah hung up the phone, she reported that Camp Horizon had been flooded! Part of its food supply was ruined. "I told the director we'd be over immediately."

The two Bobbsey men had taken Aunt Sarah's car into town and weren't expected back soon. So Aunt Sarah, the twins' mother, and the children went. They packed both families' vans with the farm's emergency supply of meat, vegetables, and fruit, and headed for the road that led directly to the site. As they had anticipated, it was rutted with mud. The campgrounds were the same, giving the place an altogether desolate look.

When she saw the visitors, Mrs. Manily, the camp director, hurried out to greet them. "May Johnny stay with us until the mud's gone?" Freddie asked quickly.

"Well, one night, anyway," Mrs. Manily agreed. While the others unloaded the vans, the woman said, "I'll get him for you."

It wasn't long before the camper came running out of one of the rear cabins.

Seeing the wet blankets strewn over railings, Aunt Sarah offered to get replacements. As she talked, Johnny leapt into the twins' van with Freddie and Flossie.

"You really are lifesavers," the camp director replied. "Thank you."

"We'll be back," Aunt Sarah promised, starting the engine.

She drove the younger children home, then continued on with the others to collect more supplies from neighbors.

In the meantime, Johnny asked the little twins, "Want to go up in the hayloft? That's where I was when your brother found me."

"Okay," Freddie agreed, and the three children climbed up the ladder.

They ran and jumped in the deep hay for a

while; then suddenly a strange expression crept over Johnny's face.

Flossie looked at him in puzzlement and Johnny put a finger to his lips. He crawled to the large opening at the end of the loft. The twins followed. When they peered through the door, they saw two men standing on the ground beneath them, talking in low tones.

Johnny pressed his lips close to the children's ears and whispered, "I'm sure those are the men I heard talking before!"

"Mitch and Oiler?" Freddie asked.

"Yes."

"Let's get them!" Quickly the children climbed down the ladder and ran out of the barn.

But evidently the men had heard them and fled. The children searched everywhere but could not find the suspects.

"We'd better tell Dinah," Flossie said.

Dinah phoned state-police headquarters, and soon two troopers arrived to investigate.

"Where's Officer Pfister?" Freddie asked.

"He doesn't work here anymore," one of the men answered. Then he asked the children to tell him everything they knew about Mitch and Oiler.

Afterward the officers made an examination of the grounds. They concluded that Mitch and

Oiler had walked from the barn to a truck on the road and taken off.

"I wish we had caught them," said Freddie. "I'll bet they were going to steal Rocket."

The troopers smiled. "You'd better leave catching them to people bigger than you," one of them advised.

As the children watched the two men leave, they sat on the back steps and looked glumly into space.

"I know something little people can do to solve a mystery!" Freddie announced.

"What?" Flossie and Johnny chimed in.

"After everybody else is asleep tonight, why don't we tiptoe downstairs and hide and wait for the piano player?"

"You mean the ghost?" Flossie asked.

"It can't be a ghost," her brother said. "Don't you remember? Dinah showed us marks on the keys."

His twin nodded. "Okay. Let's do it. But we ought to keep it a secret."

"Agreed," Freddie said. "Now, *don't* go to sleep, Flossie."

But after all the excitement, it was almost impossible for the twins to stay awake. Johnny fell asleep at once on an extra cot that had been set up in the boys' room.

Flossie dozed as well. Then she became aware of someone shaking her. "Get up!" Freddie whispered softly.

Standing alongside her, he bent to whisper again. Flossie rubbed her eyes and stepped out of bed. She put on her bathrobe and slippers and shuffled beside her brother into the moonlit hall. For the moment, everything was quiet. But as the twins reached the lower hallway, soft tinkling sounds came from the piano.

"It's spooky!" Flossie whispered. Freddie took her hand and stepped gingerly across the hall. The shadow of the pianist loomed large against the living-room wall.

More curious than ever, they peered inside. Now they could see the figure clearly. Its furry black coat shimmered in the moonlight. "Snoop!" the children cried.

The cat flew toward the kitchen, causing Flossie and Freddie to burst into laughter. Everyone except Johnny awakened and hurried to the living room.

"What's going on down here?" Uncle Daniel asked, clicking on a light.

The small twins were giggling so hard they could barely talk at first. Flossie finally said, "We caught the piano ghost!"

Freddie disappeared into the kitchen, scooped up his pet cat, and raced back. "Here he is!"

Nan and Bert grinned at each other, as Harry and the grown-ups laughed, too.

"Well, I'm glad one mystery has been solved," Dinah said with a chuckle.

The next morning at breakfast Freddie told the whole story for the benefit of Johnny.

After he was finished, Bert turned to Nan and Harry. "Are we going to let Freddie and Flossie get ahead of us as detectives?"

"No!"

"Then let's try to find Major," the boy proposed. "We know he hasn't been sold, and the men who stole him are still around, so the bull has to be around somewhere!"

■ 10 ■
Tricky Thieves

"Got any suggestions where to look?" Nan asked.

"The woods," Harry replied promptly.

"Why don't you try Hopkins Glen?" Uncle Daniel suggested. "I'll be out that way this morning. I have to see Mr. Trimble on business. Suppose you three come along."

"Maybe we can pick up a clue," Bert said.

When they were getting ready to leave, Aunt Sarah suggested they take Johnny with them. "Mrs. Manily is expecting him," she said.

Reluctantly he said good-bye to Freddie and Flossie and thanked Aunt Sarah for his visit. Then he climbed into the van.

Mrs. Manily was standing in front of her cabin when the Bobbseys pulled up. "Good morning!" she called gaily.

The children gazed at the camp in admiration. The soggy blankets had disappeared from the railings, and all the mud and debris had been removed from the ground.

"As you can see, we've been very busy," the woman said.

"The camp looks great," Nan replied.

"Thank you, dear. I hope you'll tell everyone who helped us how much we appreciate it."

Gradually, campers from every cabin ran to meet the visitors. Now they began to sing:

> We wish you a happy summer,
> We wish you a happy summer,
> We wish all the Bobbseys
> A happy summer!

The twins blushed and wished them the same, then left with Harry and Uncle Daniel. When they reached the Trimble farm, Uncle Daniel parked the van, and everyone got out. There was no sign of anyone around the dilapidated house.

"Hello!" Harry called. "Mr. Trimble?"

No one answered.

"His car is here," Uncle Daniel observed, pointing to a tiny old automobile.

"Maybe he's in the barn and can't hear us," Nan suggested.

They walked over to the ramshackle building and looked inside. It was dusky and seemed to be empty. Then they heard a muffled groan.

"Mr. Trimble!" Uncle Daniel called sharply.

"Over here," came a faint reply. "In the corner behind the wagon."

They ran to the back of the barn, where an old wagon stood loaded with bales of hay. There on the floor lay the elderly farmer.

Bert and Harry and Uncle Daniel helped Mr. Trimble to his feet.

"Thank goodness you found me!" the man exclaimed weakly. "I . . . I couldn't move!"

"What happened?" Nan asked.

"More bad luck with those two guys Mitch and Clint. They came here to the barn this morning, asking me for money. Claimed I didn't pay them what I owed them.

"I said, 'You ran off and left me empty-handed. What do you expect? Anyhow, I don't have any money.' They didn't believe me and checked all my pockets. Then Mitch got angry and hit me. The next thing I knew I was on the floor like some rusty hayfork."

"How mean!" Nan said. "Did you have any money in the house?"

"A little. I'd better see if it's still there." Harry and his father helped the man inside, and Bert and Nan followed. Mr. Trimble opened a table drawer in the kitchen.

"It's gone! My money is gone!" he said, crumpling into a chair.

"Did the men say anything else?" Bert questioned.

"Did they, Mr. Trimble?" his cousin prodded.

The farmer rubbed his forehead slowly. "Well, I did hear Clint say he was tired of hiding in the glen," he replied, "and if he had his way he'd get rid of the bull."

"Not Major!" Harry exclaimed anxiously.

"They're probably gone by now," the man said.

The children were eager to start their search. They asked Uncle Daniel to go with them, but he wanted to be sure Mr. Trimble was all right.

Bert, Nan, and Harry waited outside and felt bored. Soon Bert said, "Are there any abandoned cabins in the woods?"

"A couple," Harry answered. "Why?"

"Clint and Mitch wouldn't have stayed out in the rain if there was a cabin around."

"Good thinking," Nan said. "Where are the cabins, Hal?"

He pondered a second. "One's on top of a hill. The other is near a little stream. I think I can find it." Without telling his father, he and his cousins set off.

It seemed to the twins as if Harry were going

87

in circles. But then he called out, greatly excited, "I see the stream!"

The children followed the course of the stream, dodging fallen trees and pushing through the underbrush. After a while they saw a rough road that paralleled the water.

"The loggers must have cleared this to get the lumber out for the sawmill," Harry commented.

As the searchers quickly discovered, walking on the road made the trip easier and faster. Then suddenly Bert came to a halt.

"That looks like a cabin up ahead," he said.

"We'd better approach it from the back," Harry replied.

The small shack was between the road and the stream, so the children had little difficulty going down to the water again and creeping up from the rear.

The door was open. While Nan and Harry waited behind a tree, Bert edged forward and looked in. He turned toward the others, nodded, and walked back.

"It seems to have two rooms," he said. "The one I saw is empty, but I thought I heard someone talking in the front."

"Now what?" Nan asked. "They must be here!"

"Let's crawl up under that side window. Maybe we can hear better there."

The trio took their places under the opening. Through it filtered the voices of two men.

"When are we going to get out of here? Those kids almost caught us yesterday!" one of them complained.

"Take it easy!" a voice replied gruffly. "This is Mitch, your partner, talking. We'll go just as soon as the truck gets here."

"We'd better."

"Look, Oiler, I don't like this any more than you do. But I'm not going to leave that bull behind. And that's that."

"Follow me!" Bert said, mouthing the words.

He and the others ran a short distance into the woods and ducked behind a tree.

"We've found them!" Bert crowed triumphantly.

"But where is Major? You know he couldn't be in the house!" Harry said.

"I have a plan! We've got to work fast. Mitch said they were going to leave when the truck came. I'll scout the surrounding area to see where they hid Major. You stay here and watch the cabin. If you see the truck, get a good description."

"Be careful, Bert," Nan said.

"I will." He started toward the woods and raised two fingers in a V-for-victory sign.

Although he searched carefully among the

trees, there was no sign of the bull. "Those guys must have hidden Major *somewhere* near here!" Bert thought desperately.

Just then he noticed an odd-looking clump of withering bushes. They were unusually thick and not rooted to the ground. Creeping close to them, he spread the leaves as quietly as he could. His heart pounding like a drum, he saw a big sturdily built pen. Then his ears caught the sound of hooves pawing the ground.

"Major!" Bert thought.

He circled quickly and pushed through the bushes. Inside the pen, tossing his head and moving restlessly about, was the handsome bull!

"I have to call the troopers!" Bert said out loud.

"Not so fast, kid!"

Bert jumped. He had been thinking so hard that he had not seen the stocky sunburned man step from behind a tree. Bert recognized him instantly. He was one of the two men he had seen at the Country Diner with Officer Kent. And he was wearing a red bandanna!

"Wh-who are you?" Bert asked nervously.

"None of your business. But it looks like you've got your nose in mine. Come along!"

Bert started to run, but the burly man tripped him. Then he pulled the boy to his feet. Before Bert could yell, he clapped a hand over his

mouth and dragged him toward the cabin.

Another man was inside. Thin and wiry, he got up from a stool. "Who's that, Mitch?" he asked, glaring at Bert. "Hey, I know you."

"Y-you do?"

"Yeah, you came over to talk to Al at the diner that day."

"You sure, Oiler?" the other man put in.

"Sure I'm sure. Don't you recognize him? He's one of the Bobbsey brats." Bert sizzled but said nothing.

"Oh, now I do. I had heard you were some sort of detective," Mitch said. "When I was working for your aunt, she said you were coming for a visit. I didn't know you were a kid!"

"So you sent us a letter telling us to stay home," Bert accused. "Did you tamper with the harness on our pony cart too?"

His captor smirked. "Too bad you didn't take the hint. We only want people around who can help us," he said. "Not a bunch of nosy kids."

"Or state troopers," Bert remarked. He realized that he had turned over every damaging clue to Kent and Pfister, and they had probably destroyed all of them.

"Sit down!" Mitch barked, pushing the boy into a chair. "I caught him snooping around the bull, so I figured we ought to hold him for a while," he rasped. "Get me that rope, Oiler!"

▪ 11 ▪
Bert's Ordeal

Meanwhile, Nan and Harry had watched Bert vanish into the woods. They caught a glimpse of him every now and then as he searched among the trees. But finally he had disappeared entirely.

As time passed, Nan and Harry grew more anxious.

"Where is Bert?" Nan asked finally, her voice frantic. "I wish he'd come back!"

"He told us to stay here," Harry said. "But if we don't see him soon, I vote we go look for him!"

The minutes passed slowly. The two were just about to walk toward the cabin when they heard sounds of a scuffle.

"Oh, look!" Nan cried. "That man is taking Bert into the cabin!"

"I'll get him!" Harry said angrily, starting to run.

"No!" Nan caught her cousin by the arm. "They'll catch you, too! We've got to get Dad and Uncle Daniel!"

Harry halted. "I guess you're right, Nan. Let's go back to Trimble's."

"No," Nan said. "He's probably gone home by now. We never told him where we were going."

The two children raced down the road, crossed the stream, then cut through several fields. They ran as long as they could, until they were forced to slow down to a walk.

"I didn't realize it was so far," Nan said, panting.

"We're almost home," Harry encouraged her. "The house is just over the next hill."

They started running again and in a few more minutes collapsed breathless on the front steps of the farmhouse.

Aunt Sarah rushed out to the porch. "What's the matter?" she cried.

"Bert has been captured!" Nan managed to say.

By this time the rest of the family had reached the porch. The twins' father demanded the rest of the story quickly.

"We have to save him!" Nan finished desperately.

Mrs. Bobbsey grew pale and grasped her husband's arm. "Oh, Dick! Hurry!"

Uncle Daniel had already run into the house. In a short time he was back. "I've called the state troopers," he said, "and told them where the cabin is. They'll meet us there. Come on!"

Uncle Daniel took the family car and sped along the road toward the thieves' hideout.

"I know that logging road," Uncle Daniel remarked. "I think it joins this highway just up ahead." He swerved into a side road. The car shook as it bounced on the rough surface.

"There's the cabin!" Harry said.

Uncle Daniel slammed on the brakes. "You stay here," he instructed as the two men jumped out.

They ran into the cabin but emerged very quickly. "No one's here!" Mr. Bobbsey shouted to the children.

Now they darted inside as well. The place was completely empty! Harry raced around the side and found the pen, which was empty, too!

"They must have driven away in that truck Mitch was talking about," the boy remarked.

"And taken Bert with them!" Nan cried. "Oh, Dad!" She was almost in tears.

"Don't worry. We'll get them!" her father said grimly.

At that moment two state troopers drove up. They introduced themselves as Becker and Keller. When they learned that Mitch and Oiler had escaped, one of the officers took a deep breath.

"I suppose you know there has been a lot of cattle stealing around here lately," Becker said.

"Yes. My own bull, too," Uncle Daniel said, describing how Major had disappeared.

"We're pretty sure Mitch and Oiler are responsible," the officer continued. "But we've had a tough time proving it."

"Two of our men are working on the case undercover, pretending to help the thieves," Keller said.

"They wouldn't be Officer Kent and Officer Pfister, by any chance?" Nan asked eagerly.

"Yes, as a matter of fact."

"They came to Meadowbrook Farm to investigate," the girl detective explained, "and my brother saw Officer Kent at the Country Diner one day. He said he acted kind of strange, as if he was trying to ignore him."

"Maybe he was. Was Kent with two men?" Becker inquired.

"Yes," Harry piped up. "He was."

"Probably Mitch and Oiler," the trooper told him. "Kent didn't want to have his cover blown."

"What's the next move?" Uncle Daniel asked.

"Maybe we can pick up the truck's tire tracks," Nan spoke up.

The group searched the rough logging road in front of the cabin. "Here!" Harry said shortly.

He pointed to tracks that looked as if a large vehicle had driven in and turned around.

After examining the marks in the dirt, the troopers agreed.

"Let's see how far they go," Becker suggested.

Nan and Harry got into the trooper's car, and their fathers followed in Uncle Daniel's car. For a while the tracks were easy to follow. Several times, though, they blended into gravel but soon reappeared again.

When Becker had driven about a mile, the logging road ended at a main highway. The trooper stopped the car. "Which way now, I wonder?" he said as Uncle Daniel pulled up.

Nan, Harry, and Keller hopped out. They ran down the road, hoping to pick up the lost trail of tire tracks. But many cars and trucks had been over the same route, and it was impossible to tell one mark from another.

"Suppose we turn right," Uncle Daniel said. "Blaisdell is in that direction. The thieves may try to dispose of Major at the stock auction there."

Nan and Harry got back into the car, and Becker gunned the engine. Twenty minutes later he pulled into a gasoline station.

"I know the manager here," the trooper said. "He may have seen the bull on a truck."

"Hi, Jim!" Becker called as a jolly-faced man

strode toward him. Quickly he explained the purpose of the visit.

"I've been working on my accounts," Jim said. "I haven't paid much attention to the traffic."

They thanked the man and turned out onto the highway again. A few miles farther on, Nan suddenly pointed. "Oh! That's Bert walking up ahead!"

Mr. Bobbsey spotted him, too.

When their car drew alongside Bert, his father jumped out and gave him a big hug.

"Hi, Dad," Bert cried happily.

"It's a good thing you got away from those two," his father said.

"What happened to you?" Nan questioned as her twin climbed wearily into the troopers' car. "We saw that man drag you into the cabin, but when we got Dad and Uncle Daniel and came back, everyone was gone!"

Bert explained that his captors had tied him to a chair until a truck arrived. Then they argued about what to do with him.

"Oiler voted to leave me in the cabin," Bert said. "But Mitch was afraid someone would find me too soon. I told him I was alone, but he said that didn't matter to him. He was sure the family would miss me and spread the alarm."

He related everything the men had said, including their confession about the letter they had forged in Aunt Sarah's name. "They tried to scare us by breaking Rocket's harness," Bert revealed.

"Did you find Major?" Harry asked anxiously.

"Yes," Bert replied, "in a pen behind the cabin."

"I saw it," Harry said.

"When the men were ready to leave, they blindfolded me. They told me to climb into the cab of the truck. After that I heard them drive Major up the back ramp."

"How did you escape?" Uncle Daniel inquired.

Bert hesitated as he glanced at the troopers. "Kent and Pfister helped me. They brought the truck. I guess they're part of the gang."

Keller assured the boy that was not so. The other troopers were only pretending. They were really gathering evidence against the thieves.

Bert smiled, relieved. "They told Mitch and Oiler to let me go. They said I'd only be a nuisance to them."

"Too bad we don't have a description of the truck," Keller went on.

"I can give you one," Bert said. "I got a look at it from the cabin window before they put the blindfold on me. I saw the license plate!"

■ 12 ■
Double Returns

"Good boy!" Keller exclaimed. He jotted the license-plate number in a notebook as Bert rattled it off. "Now tell me what the truck looks like."

Since Bert had had only a partial view of it, he described it as best he could. Keller spoke into his two-way car radio and relayed the information to headquarters.

"They'll broadcast the description," the trooper explained. "We should have that truck before nightfall, unless those guys hide out someplace else."

"Won't Lieutenant Kent or Pfister contact headquarters to say where they are?" Mr. Bobbsey asked.

"If they can," Becker replied. "If they're stuck in the woods again, they won't be able to."

"Why don't you drive on home?" Keller said

to Uncle Daniel. "Take the kids with you. We'll turn up sometime."

When Uncle Daniel drove up to Meadowbrook Farm a little later, a cheer rose up from the porch. Mrs. Bobbsey, Aunt Sarah, Freddie, and Flossie all dashed down the steps and threw their arms around Bert.

"Oh, you're safe!" Flossie cried. "I was afraid the bad men would take you away forever!"

Bert chuckled, ruffling his sister's curls. "I was just playing detective like you," he teased, reporting what had happened.

As he talked, a truck rumbled into the lane. It was the same truck the thieves had used. At the wheel was Officer Kent, and next to him, Trooper Keller.

Harry and Bert hurried to greet them. "Is this your bull?" Keller asked confidently.

Harry peered into the back of the vehicle. "Major!"

"Jump in and show us where he lives," Keller said.

The cousins climbed in and directed the troopers to the barn. The ramp was lowered from the truck and Harry led the prize bull into his pen.

"Where did you find him?" Harry asked as they rode back to the house.

"You'll hear the whole story when Becker and Pfister get here. They're on their way over now, I'm happy to say, with the prisoners."

By the time Harry and Keller reached the front porch of the farmhouse, a police car was parked there. Becker was driving, with the other trooper beside him. In the back seat were Mitch and Oiler.

"Are these the men who held you in the cabin?" Becker asked Bert.

"Yes, sir," he replied. "That's Mitch," he said, pointing to the stocky, red-faced man. "And that's Oiler—his real name is Clint," Bert continued, nodding toward the other one.

"These two have been in prison before for stealing cattle. This time they were more clever about it. They claim only one cow got away."

"Lucky for Mr. and Mrs. Burns we found her," Bert revealed.

"You're one of the best detectives I know, Bert Bobbsey," Lieutenant Kent said, shaking the boy's hand.

"Thanks. Thank you very much, sir. Do you mind if I ask a question?"

"No. Go ahead."

"I still don't understand what happened to Major's hoofprints."

"Whatever evidence we found, we had to

cover up," Kent said. "Mitch and Oiler wanted to come back to the farm to try stealing more animals, and I suggested driving over the hoofprints."

"We had to prove our loyalty," his partner explained.

"No wonder you didn't want to talk to me at the diner," Bert said to Officer Kent.

"Sorry about that. I was afraid you'd create trouble for yourself."

"Thanks for identifying the crooks," Becker said to Bert as he and Pfister got into the car again. "Your timely information led to their capture. They were picked up with the stolen bull as they drove into Blaisdell."

Keller and Kent returned to the truck and followed the police car down the driveway.

"You really are wonderful detectives," Mrs. Bobbsey complimented the children.

The other grown-ups applauded.

That evening Dinah and Aunt Sarah cooked a special dinner to celebrate. The table conversation was lively, as Harry and the older twins described their adventure in detail.

"I wish we had another mystery to work on," Nan said dreamily.

"We do," Freddie said. "We still haven't found Frisky." His sister nodded sympathetically.

"Well, I may have something else for you to

do," his mother said brightly. "I had a letter this morning that concerns all of us."

"Uh-oh, another letter," Aunt Sarah said, raising her eyebrows jokingly.

"Who's it from, Mommy?" Flossie asked.

"Guess."

"Aunt Emily!" her twin brother said.

"That's riiiight!" Mrs. Bobbsey replied. "She hopes we will visit her very soon!"

Aunt Emily Minturn was Mrs. Bobbsey's sister. She lived at Ocean Cliff with her husband and their daughter, Dorothy, who was a year younger than Nan and Bert. The Bobbseys always enjoyed visiting the Minturns. To their surprise, they would soon encounter *The Secret at the Seashore.*

"We can go swimming in the ocean!" Flossie said. "I like that 'cept when the big waves knock me down!"

"When do we go?" Freddie asked, forgetting about the runaway calf.

"Not until after the County Fair," Harry spoke up, "and our farewell party."

He explained that the fair would open the following Tuesday. "We're taking Major."

Harry said the animal would need a lot of grooming to turn him into a show animal.

"Can we stay?" Bert asked his mother.

She smiled. "We can stay."

That Monday, Harry and Bert spent several hours in the barn currycombing and brushing the bull until his coat glistened. He even permitted his hooves to be painted.

"The judges will make their decisions tomorrow, and on Wednesday they'll pin the ribbons on the prize-winning animals," Harry explained. "After Dad and I get Major settled in his pen at the fair, we'll slick him up again."

Excitement ran high as everyone rode to the fairgrounds on Wednesday. At once they went to see the animal.

"Major won a blue ribbon!" Freddie exclaimed, jumping up and down. "Is that first place?"

"Yes," Nan answered. Her eyes gleamed happily. "Isn't it wonderful?"

She and the others congratulated Harry. He had taken care of Major since the bull was a calf.

Sensing that he had done something extraordinary, even Major snorted a little and pawed the ground.

"Congra-choo-la-tions, Major!" Flossie giggled.

Later, when it was time for the farewell party to begin, Aunt Sarah pinned a large picture of a bull to the big maple by the porch. "This is Major," she announced, "and the object of this game is to pin the blue ribbon on his ear!"

She passed around blue paper ribbons with a pin stuck in each. Then one by one the children were blindfolded, spun around, and given a chance to pin the ribbon on the bull. Ribbons began to decorate every part of the picture except his ear!

Bert was the last to try. He staggered and headed for the steps. "No, Bert!" Flossie squealed. "You're going the wrong way!"

The boy turned, and after a little fumbling, pinned his ribbon squarely on the bull's ear!

A round of applause went up from the onlookers.

"You can find Major every time!" Harry said with admiration.

Now there were more cheers for Bert as everyone went inside again.

"Your mom says you're leaving tomorrow," Harry told the twins. "I'm going to miss all of you. We always have real exciting adventures when you come."

"Even when we're on a picnic." Freddie giggled.

"I liked playing hide-and-seek," his sister remarked. "But I didn't like falling down the cliff!"

"Or against that old hay wagon," Harry remarked.

"Next time, Aunt Sarah," Freddie began, "can

we pick cherries?" He had had his eyes on the cherry tree in the yard.

"Why next time? You can do it right now if you like."

Quick as a bunny rabbit, he dashed outside, scrambled up to the first limb, and reached to pick a cluster of the red fruit. "Oh," he thought in dismay, "I didn't bring anything to put the cherries in."

He thought very hard. "I'll put them inside my shirt," he decided. But when there was no more room left, he began climbing down. That's when he saw an animal lope across the field.

"Frisky!" he cried.

Near the bottom now, he jumped to the ground but lost his balance. *Splat!* The boy landed with a loud thump, facedown.

"What was that?" Flossie asked. She was in the kitchen with Nan.

Her sister gaped through the window, horrified. Freddie was lying motionless in a pool of red liquid! "Freddie!" she cried, hurrying everyone outside.

Flossie screamed the minute she saw him, too, which made the boy sit up, though somewhat unsteadily. "Stop screaming," he said. "I'm okay."

"But you're bleeding!" his twin insisted.

"It's not blood," Nan corrected. "It's cherry juice!"

"I smashed all my cherries! But look what I found!" He pointed to the silky black-and-white calf in the distance.

"Frisky came back!" Flossie exclaimed.

By now Harry had also seen Frisky and was coaxing her toward the barnyard.

As the children watched in fascination, Aunt Sarah said, "Do you realize that every Bobbsey has gotten into trouble except Nan?"

"I'm just lucky," she said shyly.

"Think so, dear?" her mother asked, looking at Nan's feet.

Unwittingly, the girl had stepped into the cherry juice and splattered it all over her white sandals!

"Whoops! Oh, well." Nan laughed. "What's a mystery without trouble for *all* the Bobbsey twins!"